NED'S NEW FRIEND

DAVID EZRA STEIN

A PAULA WISEMAN BOOK

SIMON & SCHUSTER BOOKS FOR YOUNG READERS

NEW YORK LONDON TORONTO SYDNEY

SIMON & SCHUSTER BOOKS FOR YOUNG READERS
An imprint of Simon & Schuster Children's Publishing Division
1230 Avenue of the Americas, New York, New York 10020

SIMON & SCHUSTER BOOKS FOR YOUNG READERS is a trademark of Simon & Schuster, Inc.
Book design by Einav Aviram
The text for this book is set in ITC Clearface.
The illustrations for this book are rendered in ink and watercolor.
Manufactured in China
2 4 6 8 10 9 7 5 3 1
Library of Congress Cataloging-in-Publication Data
Stein, David Ezra.
Ned's new friend / David Ezra Stein. — 1st ed.
p. cm.
"A Paula Wiseman book."
Summary: When Cowboy Ned meets Miss Clementine, his horse, Andy,
who is his best friend, becomes jealous.
ISBN-13: 978-1-4169-2490-6 (hardcover)
ISBN-10: 1-4169-2490-6 (hardcover)
[1. Jealousy—Fiction. 2. Friendship—Fiction. 3. Behavior—Fiction.
4. Cowboys—Fiction. 5. Horses—Fiction.
6. West (U.S.)—Fiction.] I. Title.
PZ7.S8179Cox 2007
[E]—dc22
2006010582

In memory of my dad

Cowboy Ned and his best buddy, Andy, reached the end of the trail at Abilene Town.

Ned bought a new shirt. Andy had his hooves oiled.

They had just left the general store with two full-to-the-brim
root beer floats when a lovely lady came along.

Ned missed a step—what a disaster!

The lady came over to offer her hankie. "Are you all right, Mister—?"

"Ned," said Ned. He turned red as a sunset.

"Well, Mr. Ned, you're welcome to return this sometime tomorrow. Come to the yellow house and ask for Miss Clementine."

"I-I-I—thank you," Ned managed at last.

At bath time Ned was still clutching the hankie.

Before bed he folded it carefully and put it under his pillow.
The lullaby he sang that night was different. Instead of the song
about the happy roving cowboy, Ned sang a new song about a
girl in a shady grove.

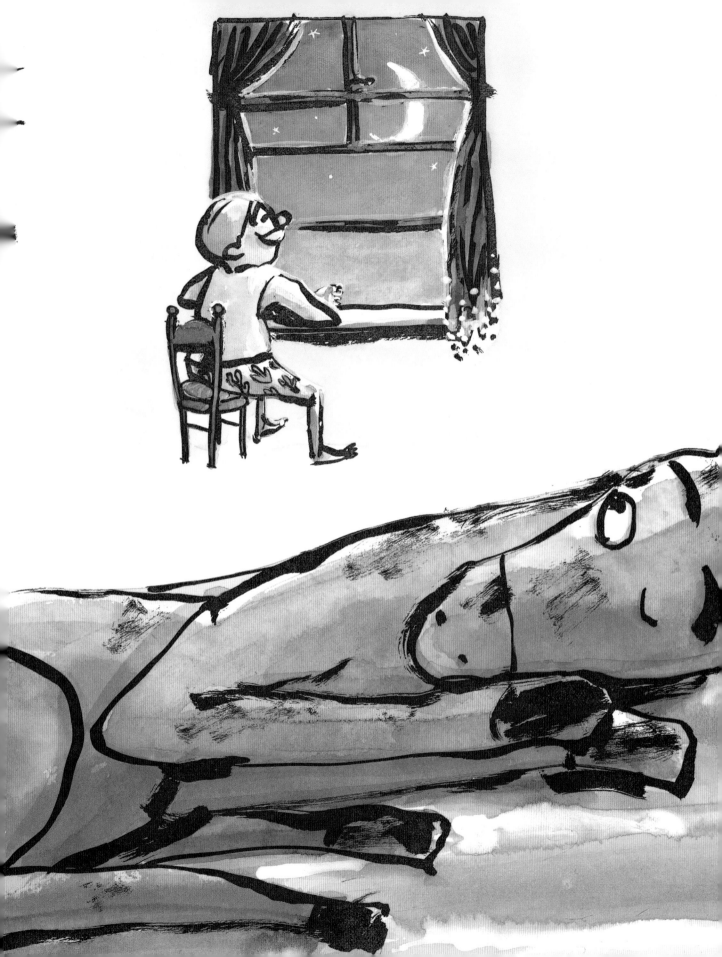

That night Andy dreamed he was running as fast as he could. Ned and Clementine were sailing away in a big, beautiful balloon, and he was trying to keep up with them.

Before he could catch up, the balloon sailed away into the clouds where Andy couldn't follow.

When Andy woke up, it was still night. *That hankie is bad news,* he thought. *If I get rid of it, everything will be back to normal.*

With dainty lips, Andy rooted under Ned's pillow and nabbed the hankie. He took it over to the open window.

The hankie seemed to be soaked in perfume, so just as he was thinking, *Maybe this is the wrong thing to do*—"Achoo!" The hankie swooped out into the night.

Meanwhile two robbers were sneaking around Abilene with bags of loot.

Lefty was sulking, looking at the ground, because he fancied he'd got less loot than Righty. Then he spied the hankie and gleefully tied it on his face. *Just like a real robber,* he thought.

As they got down to the train tracks to escape out east, Righty heard the sheriff's deputy following them, so they hid. Lefty was scared. "Maybe this was the wrong thing to do–oo–achoo!" He sneezed. "This hankie!" he said, tossing it aside.

At that, the deputy found them and put them in jail.

The hankie sat beside the rails until the 12:33 out of Gopher City whipped past and blew it high into the air. . . . And wouldn't you know, it landed in the roses that grew at Miss Clementine's gate.

The next day Ned and Andy came to call on Miss Clementine.

Ned was looking anxiously at the ground, wondering how he would explain the missing hankie.

Andy was watching the sky for balloons.
That was when he saw the hankie.

For a moment he pretended not to see it. *Maybe it will blow away and keep on blowing,* he thought. *And things will be like they were.*

Then he looked hard at it. *But then Ned would never find it, and he'd be sad forever. And I'd never have the old Ned back.*

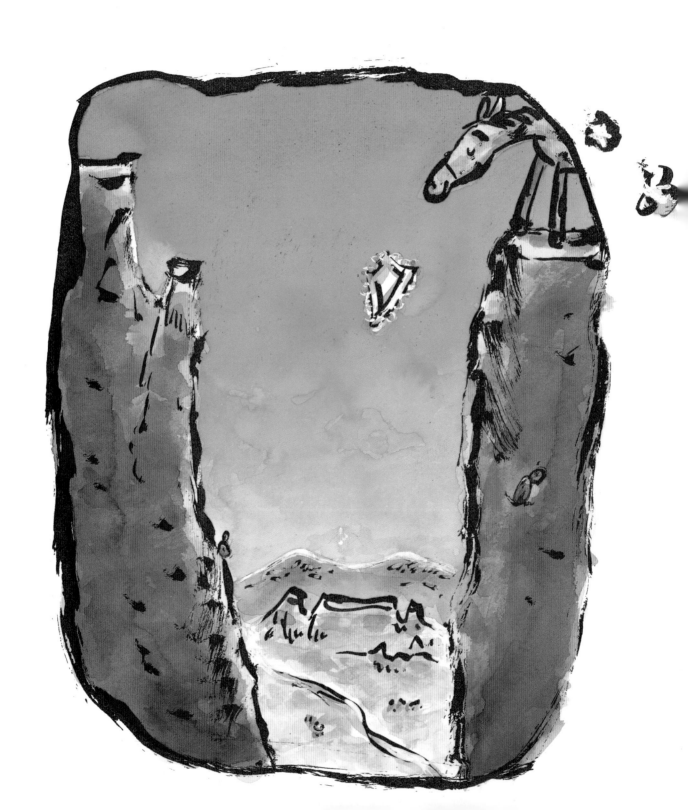

Then he knew what he had to do. *Ned wants that hankie, and I am going to give it to him, no matter what,* he thought. *Because a happy Ned is the kind of Ned I want.*

And that's what he did.

Ned broke into a grin. "I don't know how you did it, old buddy, but you saved the day," he whispered, and knocked on the door.

Miss Clementine answered. "Why if it isn't Mr. Ned," she said. "And who's this fine young horse by your side?"

"Miss Clementine," said Ned, "may I introduce my best friend in the whole world: Andy."

Andy blushed.

"Pleased to meet you, Andy," said Clementine. "I think I made just enough cookies for three. Won't you two come in and have some tea?"

And they did.

And Andy thought that was fine.